T.T. HARRIS

I0551205

When the heart becomes
entangled with what is right,
there are...

LEGAL
PROBLEMS

This book was printed in the United States of America.

To order additional copies of this book, visit:
Email: thekeysproductions@gmail.com
www.thekeysproductions.com

Acknowledgements

First, I want to thank God for my life and the ability to be creative.

To my parents, thank you for sending me to school and never accepting the minimum from me. Mom and daddy, you required that I do EVERYTHING with a spirit of excellence and I believe this novel is excellence at its best.

To my husband, E. Nathan Harris, you are my heartbeat and have been so patient with all of the nights I was up staring at the computer, texting and emails. Thank you for all the prayers and consistent reminders that I am gifted and anointed for the work. Life would be so boring without you. I love you honey bear.

To my children, thank you for allowing me to parent the best kids in the world.

To my brothers, thank you for all the tough love and encouraging me.

To my best friends, Tisa, Angie, Syreeta, and Erica; I never thought those nights when we were kids having sleepovers and making up silly stories, I would be a published author today. Thank you for encouraging me with your insight and knowledge to strive beyond the basics. Thank you for reading my random ideas and telling me when they needed improvement.

To my web designer and publication partner, Tamika Hall – CEO of El Shaddai Productions, thank you for all the hard work you put into making my dream come true. You spent months working with me and fighting with me because I'm stubborn (smile). You pushed me to think outside of the box and to reach for the stars. I am eternally grateful to you I pray that God blesses you beyond measure.

To my readers and supporters, I hope you enjoy this novel and will support my series of books I will be releasing soon. Without you there is no me.

To my sister, Shandolen, I'm looking for the words to express my heart and all I can think of is the last thing you told me before you went to sleep; you said to me, "If no one believes in you, I do. I believe in you." Those words comfort my heart on some of the toughest times I have in my life. And inspire me to be the best woman I can be not only for myself but for you too. I dedicate my first published work to your legacy and memory. I will always love you forever. "Make ya'll day count!"

Chapter One

Michael and Tasha Davis were excited about their new move from Atlanta to Chicago. After finishing top in his law school class, he was offered a job working as a human rights attorney. Tasha is a successful small business consultant. Michael and Tasha arrive in a black town car in front of a luxurious high-rise apartment complex. The moving trucks were already there unloading their new furniture and items that were shipped from Atlanta.

"Oh my, God, Michael," Tasha gushes looking around; "this place is so amazing. This all seems like a dream to me."

Michael grabs his briefcase and a few boxes. Tasha grabs her plants and the door man greets them. They stand in the large vest view and look at the beautiful paintings, sculptures, and marble ceiling. As they walk into the elevator and Michael bumps directly into a woman and drops his briefcase.

She reaches down and picks the briefcase up and Michael says, "I'm sorry. I didn't see you."

Paulette responds, "It's all good. I didn't see ya'll walk in. How you doing? My name is Paulette."

Michael looks her up and down and notices her tattoos on her arms and pierced tongue. He gives a sarcastic grin and says, "Hello, I'm Michael and this is my wife, Tasha."

Paulette looks at Michael with a half smile and turned to Tasha and says, "Welcome to the neighborhood. I'm sure you will love it in the Baldwin Towers. I live in apartment 21E. If you need anything, please let me know. I know the best markets to shop at."

Tasha smiles and says, "That sounds great! We live a few floors up from you but, I'm sure we will run into you again. Not literally of course. And yes it would be great to have a tour to shop and buy groceries. We're from Atlanta and don't know anyone here. Thank you again, Paulette."

The doors open to the elevator and Paulette jumps out and

throws her hand up to say good bye, "Please call me, Paulie, I prefer that better."

Tasha waves back and the doors close. Michael frowns at his wife and with a stern voice roughly says, "I don't like her. She seems too friendly."

Tasha laughs at Michael and steps off the elevator. They stand in front of the doors to their success. The apartment doors were already open and the movers had just finished unloading everything. The Davis' look around the apartment in total awe of how much space there is. The penthouse apartment overlooks the city skyline. Michael walks across the hardwood floors into the living room and flops down on the cozy leather couch. He props his foot up on the coffee table and says, "This is why I worked so hard, baby, in school."

Tasha comes behind him and wraps her arms around his neck, "I thought you worked this hard to get me to marry you." They both share a laugh and Michael turns around to kiss Tasha.

He responds, "That's the other reason why. Gosh, it seems

like yesterday when I first met
you." Michael starts reminiscing of
his college years and precious
moments with Tasha.

*Tasha and Michael met in
college while attending Morehouse
College and Spellman College. The two
fell in love at a basketball game when
Michael went to make a play on a loose
ball and landed in Tasha's lap on the
side line.*

*"Wow, I am so sorry. Are you
ok?" Michael says as he jumps off of the
young lady who was blushing. Tasha
was so embarrassed yet she was excited
that the star player of Morehouse
College landed in her lap. She giggled
and said, "I'm ok. You did manage to
sweat on me. So, in exchange for this
awkward moment you can treat me to a
soda after the game." Tasha got up with
her friends and walked away. Michael
stood in pure amazement of this
beautiful woman who made his heart
skip a beat. He yells at her as she
walked away,*

*"What's your name and where
do I meet you?" Tasha says, "Ask my
frat brothers on your team. They know
where to find me." Michael finished the
game with a career high in scoring and
assists for the season. But, his mind*

was fixed on finding this woman who was so intriguing. He asked around to the other players on the team and they told him her name was Tasha Johnson. They laugh and said he didn't have a chance with her because was dating someone already. However, Michael was determined to win her heart. Michael found Tasha sitting in the pizza shop down the street from her school. He walked in feeling like he had complete control and as soon as he saw her he got nervous and walked out.

Michael talks to himself, "What is wrong with me. She's a girl and I have dated plenty of girls. I got this." His heart is pounding so fast he wonders if she can hear it has he walks back into the shop and to her table. He sits down in the booth next to her and stumbles over the words to say. Finally, he mumbles out, "Would you like your soda now? I can go get you one like you asked."

Tasha smiles and says, "No, I don't want a soda. I was just playing with you but I'm glad you did your research and found me. You had an awesome game tonight despite you throwing yourself into my lap to get my attention." Michael couldn't help but to smile and said, "I really didn't see you but I'm glad I fell on you. So, what's up? I heard you got a man. When you going to break up with him and marry me?" Tasha's face turned red and lost her breath. Tasha didn't expect Michael to make such a bold statement. It was such a turn on to her and wondered if she's wasting her time dating and should consider Michael.

"Well aren't you very confident that you can have me or even handle me. What makes you think I want you? I don't even know you like that and besides you could have a reputation of being a player."

Michael was a little shocked by her words and said in sincerity in his voice, "I have never been a player. I only date one woman at a time. I haven't been with anyone since I got to school here. Coming from Texas, my parents raised me to be a gentleman and respect myself and women. So, I'm waiting on the right woman and she just may be you. With that said, I would like to formally ask you go on a date this Friday night. Could I treat you to dinner and a movie?" Tasha tucked her head to the side and replied, "Yes, I would like that very much."

After a year of dating, graduation, law school and a short engagement, Michael and Tasha jumped the broom and right into their new life together as husband and wife.

"Michael, we need to find a grocery store so I can get some food and make dinner." Michael rose from the couch and kissed Tasha. "Honey, I want to take you out for a nice dinner and sightseeing tonight. So, get your prettiest dress and those red heels I love." Tasha sprints to the master bedroom to look through her boxes and prepare for her night out. Michael felt his phone vibrate and looks at the email alert he received from the office.

Chapter Two

Welcome to Chicago Michael from West Miller and associates. Please report into the office at 8:00am for a morning briefing and be prepared to stay until at least six o' clock.

"Hey honey, I just got an email about what time I need to be in the office tomorrow. I should be home around six o'clock at the latest."

I'm so nervous but at the same time excited about the next step in my life. Are you almost ready?" Tasha walked out the bedroom with her red flowing dress and red shoes. She answered with a seductive voice, "do I look ready to you baby?"

Michael stepped in front of Tasha and grabs her into a big bear hug. "You look fabulous babe. Let's go! I'm so hungry right now. That plane food did nothing for me." Tasha and Michael left for a romantic night on the town and followed it with making love for the first time in their new home.

The next morning, a chorus of "Good morning, Mr. Davis," filled the office from different colleagues and the secretaries sitting in front of each office. Michael smiled from ear to ear with the joy of being welcomed. It eased the nervousness he was feeling. In his office, he was pleasantly surprised to find a large cherry wood desk and cozy chair. Law books are all lined up on the shelves. It looked like a library. The large bay window overlooked the city and Michael stood in front of it gazing in the happiness of his new future.

A soft knock interrupted his thoughts.

"Come in." Michael says.

The partners of the firm, Mr. Miller and Mr. West came in to welcome Michael to Chicago and to the firm. Mr. Miller sat on the couch and says, "I'm so glad you took our offer over the many ones you received. We at Miller, West and Associates are ecstatic to have you working with us. I'm sure you will fit in very well with the firm. Here are your keys to the fitness center, private washroom and office. Also, here is your key pass card to enter in and out of the building after office hours."

Mr. West chimed in, "David, don't overwhelm him on the first day. He needs a chance to get adjusted here. However, I do expect you in the morning meeting and we are having cocktails and poker this Friday night in the penthouse suite. It's our monthly poker night and our getaway from the women." All the gentlemen laughed out loud as Mr. West and Mr. Miller left the office.

Just as Michael sat down to look over some materials, his phone buzzed.

"Yes Shauntel." Michael said, with a smile on his face, he was so excited to actually have a secretary.

"Mr. Davis, your nine o'clock appointment is here," Shauntel said in a chipper voice.

"Thank you, please send him in," Michael said and steadied his nervous breath. This is what he had gone to school for all of these years, but school could never prepare one for what it means to accept their first client.

A slender, brown-skinned man walked in. His cologne filled the office as he shook Michael's hand and introduced himself,

"Good morning, my name is Jeffrey."

"Have a seat Jeffrey, my name is Michael and I will be representing you in court," Michael said in his most confident voice. "Where would you like to begin?"

"I don't really know where to start," Jeffrey said quietly.

"How about you tell me a little about yourself," Michael prodded as he unbuttoned his suit jacket to sit down.

"Well, I'm thirty years old. I'm from Chicago, and I work as a registered nurse at Chicago Memorial downtown," Jeffrey took a brief breath before continuing, "I'm working towards finishing school to become a doctor. I don't have any family here. I'm originally from Richmond, VA. Oh, and I'm gay. Did they tell you anything about my case?" Jeffery finished his ramblings and looked to Michael for a reaction.

Michael tried not to look as is if he had swallowed a bird. He couldn't believe that this professional man was gay and so open about it! Clearing his throat he cautiously answered, "Well, no they didn't tell me anything about your case." He stares at Jeffrey a moment. "You don't look gay."

"What is gay supposed to look like?" Jeffrey said with an astonished look on his face.

"I didn't mean to offend you." Michael says quickly, "I just thought that most gay men look a certain way. I really haven't been around any gay men before. Please excuse my ignorance." Michael said apologetically.

"It's okay, I'm not offended. I just like to inform people that they shouldn't judge a book by its cover without reading it first." Jeffrey assessed Michael for a moment. His piercing gaze made Michael a little uneasy and he fought to control his feelings. "Would you like me to tell you why I'm here today?" Jeffrey finally finished.

"Please, I'm curious to know."

Jeffrey stood up and began pacing the room. "I'm here because I was violently raped by a man that I thought I was in love with."

Michael looked shocked, "Are you serious? Is that even possible?"

"Yes, it's very possible and my life hasn't been the same since." Jeffrey answered indignantly. It happened a year ago. I was in Los Angeles for a medical conference. After a session, I was having a drink in the bar of the hotel where the conference was. A guy sat down next to me and asked why I was there. I looked at him and he was so beautiful. His skin was like chocolate and his eyes were as bright as the sun."

Michael swallowed hard as he listened to this recounting of the meeting. He takes out a notepad began to make notes, partly because it was the professional thing to do, and the other part was to give him a reason to stay calm as he listened to his client.

"I told him I was there for the conference and he replied that he was too. He asked me if I would like to join him to continue our drink in his room. I didn't think twice about that. I followed him to his room. We sat down on the couch and opened the wine and talked. It seemed like I'd known him for years. I left his room feeling good about meeting someone so nice."

"The next day we sat next to each other at the session. We just kept looking at each other and before I knew it, I was in his room at lunchtime on my knees giving him a blow job. His body was perfect."

Michael was so into the story that he stopped writing notes and closed his eyes to listen to Jeffery. "We had already unclothed each other as we hit the door. It was so good, when he was ready to release, he told me to get on my back and he did it on my chest. I hadn't had anyone do that to me before."

Michael began to get aroused and the sweat began to pour from his forehead. "Ma...Maybe we should stop there for the day and reconvene tomorrow at nine o'clock." Michael stuttered as he gathered himself and led Jeffrey to the door.

Luckily, Jeffrey left without a fuss, but Michael was troubled by the conversation he had had with Jeffrey. He tried to bury himself into his case reviews but, all he could seem to think about was Jeffrey telling his story.

Michael left work exhausted and
confused.

Chapter Three

"**Honey,** I'm home."
Michael said as he kicks off his
shoes and headed straight for the
refrigerator to get a beer.

"Are you okay?" Tasha asked
Michael a look of concern on her
face. "You look like you had a really
rough first day."

Opening his beer Michael
decided to be honest, "I did. My
client is gay and I have to represent
him. He said that his lover violently
raped him. Can you believe that? I
didn't think that was possible. The
things some people will say."

"Do you think he deserved
what happened to him?" Tasha
asked with a disturbed look on her
face.

Annoyed by Tasha's tone,
Michael watched Tasha wash the
dishes. He listens to clanging sound
for a moment before answering,
"No, I don't think people no matter
what gender they are should be
violated. That's why I'm going to
put as much effort and compassion
into this case to help him win."

"Well, the only way you're
going to be able to understand your

client is to place your feet in the man's shoes. Then you will really know how he feels and maybe you will have more sympathy for him." Tasha countered. "Think about it this way honey, this is a new job for you and with that comes new challenges. You'll be able to conquer this once you accept that this is just one of those all things new type of deals."

Michael watched the gentle sway of Tasha's hips as she scrubbed a pot. She was beautiful without even trying. He wanted to run his hands over the curves of her body bury his lips into her sweet smelling neck and press his manhood into the softness of her behind. He couldn't help be wonder how a man could ever want to be anywhere else other than on top of a woman.

Running his hands under her dress, he quickly turned her around. She immediately wrapped her suds filled hands around his neck and he lifted her onto the edge of the sink.

"Michael?" Tasha whispered questioning his intentions.

"Shhh" he silenced her with a kiss. "Remember, this all things new, right?"

He smiled at her as he entered and they experienced the sturdiness of their kitchen counter for the first time.

Chapter Four

After two weeks of working closely with Jeffrey, Michael began to feel comfortable with his work and being around Jeffrey. He couldn't explain it, but he felt a closeness that he hadn't felt since college.

The next morning, on this particular morning, Michael rushed out of the apartment without breakfast to get a jumpstart on his game plan. While fixing his shirt, tie and freshening his cologne, a knock sounded at the door.

"Right on time," Michael said under his breath looking at his watch to see that it was nine o'clock on the dot.

"Good morning, Jeffrey," Michael said shaking his hand.

Smiling Jeffrey responded to Michael by saying, "Please call me Jeff. We don't need to be that formal anymore. It has been weeks since I've been coming here."

"I wanted to show you some receipts of things that I purchased while Malik was staying with me"
"I want to get back everything I put

into that relationship. Look at all these bills he left me with. I went into debt while I was in the hospital and he just moved on with his life as if it was just a break up."

Michael could see the hurt and frustration on Jeffrey's face as it turned red.

"He insisted on us spending a lot of time at my apartment in Chicago because he said his roommate was always around and we wouldn't have any privacy. I should've known then that it something was wrong." Michael watched Jeffrey as he paced the floor.

"The first time we made love was after a weekend of dinner and theater. He made me feel so special and I wanted to do anything I could to keep him in my life." Jeffrey reached in his pocket for his handkerchief to wipe his eyes. "He was so gentle that night. He made sure that the mood was perfect and that I was comfortable. It felt so good to me and I couldn't contain my happiness. His body was flawless and he was the right size to get the job done. I know this might sound strange to you but it was like when you've had sex for the first time with someone you love. I let him move in with me after he told me that he would transfer to the hospital here to do his research. I was so excited about having him with me all the time."

It was only after a few months that I noticed we were getting collection notices all the time. I couldn't figure out where the money was going too. I did some research of my own and found out some awful things about Malik. The apartment that he supposedly had wasn't his at all. It was his ex-boyfriend's place and he was staying on his couch. The clothes and the money that he had were all borrowed. He lied about transferring to work here. He would leave before me and wait at a bar down the street for about two hours when he knew I was gone and come back home. All he did was lie on the couch with a beer in one hand and the remote control in the other. So, I surprised him one afternoon and came home early. I confronted him about the lies and asked him to pack his things and leave. He left but he made sure to tell me that I would pay for treating him the way I did."

Michael gave Jeffrey a moment to collect himself, "are you able to continue or do you want to reschedule?"

"No, I need to get closure," Jeffrey took a deep breath."

About a month went by and I went out to celebrate passing all of my exams with some friends of mine. I shared a cab with a friend and he walked to my door because I was very tipsy from the drinks. I didn't know that Malik was waiting in his car for me to get home. He saw my friend give me a hug and get back in the cab.

As I opened my apartment door, I felt a fist in the back of my head. He started punching me and screaming that he would kill me. He pinned me down and ripped my scrub bottoms and began ramming me uncontrollably. All I could do is yell for help. I couldn't get him off of me and he knew that. Even after I started bleeding, he still didn't stop until he released on me. I was covered in my own blood and his semen. He zipped his pants, stole my wallet and ran out of the apartment as fast as he could. He even pushed a lady coming up the stairs while he was coming down. She saw my door open and walked in to see me lying there battered, bruised and humiliated. She called the police and an ambulance.

I was in the hospital for two weeks recovering from a torn anal area, a broken nose and bruised kidneys. The doctors told me that I wouldn't be able to have anal sex again from the complications that I suffered and not to mention that using the restroom is very painful."

Michael stood up and walked toward Jeffrey. Michael tried not to let the shock he felt show on his face as he said, "I am here for you. I just want you to know that I will do everything I can to get you justice."

"Thanks, Man," Jeffrey said. "That is all I ask from you."

Standing up Michael decided he needed to lighten the mood, "Look, after having such a long session, I'm in the mood for a beer. Would you like to join me after work?"

Smiling Jeffrey said "Yes, I would like that very much. So, I will meet you here at six o'clock?"

Michael nodded his head "yes" as he picked up his phone to make a call Jeffrey let himself out of the office.

"Hey, Baby," Michael said with love in his voice when Tasha picked up the phone, "I'm going to get a drink after work with Jeff. I wanted to give you a heads up so you won't be looking for me."

"Okay, Mike, I'll see you when you get home," Tasha answered. "Honey, just don't be too late, because your wife will be waiting for here at home."

"No, baby, I won't be long. You want me to pick you up something to eat?"

"No, baby, you misunderstood me." Tasha said with a short laugh. "I don't need you to bring me anything on the menu, because I plan on being on the dessert menu."

"Oh," Michael thought about her statement for a moment before he understood what she was saying. His manhood tightened with desire to be inside of his beautiful wife. "Tasha, I'm on my way home." He hung up the phone to her musical laughter. All he

could think about was the
"Afternoon Delight" that was
waiting for him at home.

Chapter Five

Six o'clock, Michael was waiting at the front of the building for Jeffrey to arrive. Buttoning his coat, he wondered if he was doing the right thing. It was one thing to represent someone in "the lifestyle" in a courtroom, but it was something all together different to go out with him to a bar. What if someone saw them together? Would they think he was gay also?

Michael had just put on his hat to cover his freshly shaven head when Jeffrey arrived. Smiling, Jeffrey said, "The bar is only three blocks up the street. We can walk if you want to."

Patting his stomach, Michael responded, "That's fine. I haven't worked out since I been here. I feel a little fat these days."

Jeffrey quickly ran his eyes over Michael's physique, "You look good to me," He said with adoration in his voice.

Michael couldn't help but blush as they began to walk.

They open the door to a small Irish pub and see that there are only a few people in the bar. They take

off their coats and sit down. A
waiter takes their order and leaves
some peanuts on the table as he
walks away. Michael grabs a hand
of peanuts to crack the shells.

He begins the conversation
by saying, "You know I want to
share something with you that I
haven't told anyone not even Tasha.
I had an experience with a guy that
changed me too. He didn't rape me
but, he made me feel so good
emotionally and sexually. I blocked
it from my mind because of my
convictions. I never really got over
it. He was my first and sometimes I
wonder what would have
happened if we didn't break it off. I
was young then but, I'm old
enough to handle whatever comes
my way now." Jeffrey says, "Do
you really think you can handle
having buried feelings surface and
not want to explore the possibilities
again or are you really happy being
married?"
Michael looks somewhat
confused. Yet he was very
interested in where this
conversation was going. He says, "I

know I can handle it. The question
is can you handle me?"

Jeffrey smiles and says, "Oh,
I know I can handle you." They
stare at each other with such a
sexual intensity.

Then, Michael tries to change
the subject. "I can tell my wife is a
little upset with me about how
much time I'm spending in the
office already. When I get home, all
can think about is you. I mean the
case."

Jeffrey replies, "It's okay to
think about me. It's not like I don't
think about you. I wonder how
your day is going and how
fortunate I am to have you here for
me. I wish there was a chance to
share my gratitude for all you have
done for me."

Michael leans back in the
chair and says, "There is a way for
you too. You can be my workout
partner. We will go to the gym
every other day before work. How
does that sound?" Jeffrey looks
pleased and says, "I would love to
be your partner.

They leave and walk about
two blocks and end up at Michael's
apartment. Michael puts out his

hand for Jeffrey to shake and he pulls him in close and whispers, "I'll see you in the morning for a workout." Jeffrey could feel Michael's lips grazing his ear. It sent a chill to his body.

Michael arrives home to see Tasha laying on the couch napping. He kisses her forehead and heads towards the bathroom to take a shower. He stood under the running water and his mind reminisced on the conversation he had with Jeffrey.

Tasha heard the water running and decided to light some candles in the bedroom and open up a bottle of wine to set the mood. She took off his basic pajamas and put on a sexy red laced gown that hugged the curves of her beautiful chocolate body to increase the ambiance for the evening.

Michael walks out of the steamy bathroom to see Tasha lying across the bed motioning him to come over to her. Michael dropped his towel and climbed into their California king sized bed. He kissed Tasha passionately and caressed her body as though he longed for this moment.

"Michael, what has gotten into you, Tasha says as he turns her over on her stomach." Michael enters his wife and begins to stroke gently. Michael's mind wanders to his conversation with Jeffrey and he remembers feeling Jeffrey's ear as he touched him with his lips. Michael begins to stroke harder, He imagined Jeffrey and thought about how it would feel to be inside of him. Michael started shaking and thrusting his body into Tasha. At first, Tasha was enjoying the moment but then she noticed that Michael wasn't himself and he was rougher than usual. He began to talk dirty to her and curse at her.

"You like it hard like that babe? How you loving this big black dick! Let me bang your back out bitch!"

Tasha raises her voice in confusion, "Michael, you're hurting me. Why are you doing this to me?"

"What are you talking about, honey? It doesn't feel good to you?"

Tasha pushed Michael out of her, sat up and angrily replied, "No, it didn't feel good and I didn't like the way you talked to me. You

never disrespected me like that and
you better not ever do it again."

Tasha rolled out of bed and
glared at Michael as she went to the
bathroom to calm down. Michael
sat at the edge of the bed and held
his head in disbelief of what had
just taken place.

Chapter Six

The next morning, Michael grabs his bag and heads directly to the gym without saying anything to Tasha. Tasha gathers herself and decides to explore the windy city. "I don't know where I'm going. Maybe I should just knock on Paulie's door and see if she wants to hang out."

Just as she arrives at Paulie's door, Paulie and her girlfriend walk out of their apartment carrying a beautiful gray teacup Yorkie in a Louis Vuitton bag.

Tasha smiles and says, "Wow Paulie, you're dog is so cute!" I always wanted a Yorkie but they are more high maintenance than me. I'm sorry to bother you but I was about to wander around to find some places to shop and blow off some steam and figured I would see if you're free today."

Paulie's girlfriend stops in her tracks and says, "Baby, who is this and why are you looking like you've been caught?"

Paulie responded angrily, "First of all, Jazz; watch your mouth talking to me like that. Tasha and

her husband Michael just moved in
upstairs a few weeks ago. Tasha,
please excuse my jealous soon to be
ex girlfriend Jazz." Jazz's face
slumped in embarrassment and fear
that Paulie was serious about her
being an ex girlfriend. Paulie saw
how embarrassed and sad Jazz had
gotten. She grabbed her arm and
pulled her close to kiss her.
        "Boo, you know I was
playing. But, please don't do that
again."
        Tasha extended her hand to
shake Jazz's hand. She smiled
gracefully and says, "Nice meeting
you Jazz. Paulie was so nice to me
and I'm sure we all will be good
friends."
        Jazz agreed and the three
ladies walked out the apartments
towards the subway. Paulie noticed
Tasha's hesitation going towards
the subway. "Tasha, I assure you
the subway is safe. I know you're
not from here but you're gonna to
have to get used to it unless you
want to spend a lot of money on
cabs or parking garages. I barely
ever drive my car. And, I save a lot
of money traveling this way. Where
is your husband this morning? I

could tell he didn't take to kindly of me from the way he looked at me. It's cool. I usually don't get along with men anyway, especially bisexual or men on the down low."

Tasha looked perplexed and asked, "What are you talking about? My husband is neither one of them. He is as straight as they come." Paulie snickered and says, "Are you sure about that? Listen sweetie, I have been around a lot of people in my life and one thing I know when a man has been with another man or is thinking about it. I was only around your husband for a quick elevator ride and he gave me some shade and straight men don't do that. Let me guess, did he tell you he didn't like me?"

Tasha sadly said, "Yes, how did you know that?" My husband isn't on the down low. Sure he likes to dress up and is very sensitive but that doesn't mean he gets down like that. Besides if he ever did, he would've told me. I think he would have told me. Shoot, I don't care if he did, that would be his past. However, I would be pissed if he didn't tell me."

Jazz chimed in and says, "Paulie, stop putting those crazy thoughts in her head. Tasha, don't pay her any attention. She thinks everybody is gay or has had experiences like that before. She can't face the fact that the whole world isn't curious."

The women chuckled and started talking about shopping and lunch. In the back of Tasha's mind she wondered if Paulie was right.

As Michael arrived to the athletic club, he saw Jeffrey running towards the door to meet him. Michael began to smile and wave at him. As the two men went into the crowded gym, they found a quiet corner at the east wing of the gym that had the stationary bicycles. Michael watched Jeffrey as he mounted the bicycle and was mesmerized by the motion of his body.

"Wow, Jeff, your legs look amazing. How long have you been working out? From the looks of your body you must live in the gym."

Jeffrey giggled and replied, "Chile please. My body ain't all that. I walk a lot because of my work and barely get a good meal because of all the 12- hour shifts I work regularly. So, I don't get a chance to get to the gym as much as I would like. And I wasn't motivated until now." Jeffrey arched his back on the bike to show his toned body. He bounced up and down to lure Michael's attention. Michael's face lit up and he was staring uncontrollable at him. Michael decided to make small talk to stop himself from being so obvious he was attracted to Jeffrey's body.

"Well, I need to get myself together. I used to play basketball all the time but, after I got married Tasha monopolized my time with shopping, watching movies and networking with business clients. I really thought I would be in the pros playing but after I blew my knee out in college, I got discouraged and didn't have the support to go back and play again." Michael sits down next to the bike and slumps over. His face looked as if he lost his best friend. Jeffrey notices that Michael isn't smiling and looks unhappy. He sits next to him and puts his arm around Michael's shoulder. Jeffrey thinks of the best words to comfort Michael and says,

"Why the long face, Boo? Listen, you can always play basketball again. There are plenty of adult leagues in Chicago and I'm sure you will be great again. Never give up on your dreams despite people not supporting you. I learned that a long time ago and when I stopped focusing on people and thinking about myself I found that my life was more fulfilled." Michael looked Jeffrey in the face and was fascinated by his knowledge and wisdom.

"Damn, you really made me feel so much better and I think I will look into playing basketball again. Thank you for the encouragement. My wife hasn't even done that for me. You are so amazing." Michael looks at his watch and realizes he's been at the gym longer than he anticipated. He stands up and motions to Jeffrey to follow him to the shower. The steam filled the shower room as they walked in.

Michael began to look closely at Jeffrey's brown body as the water makes a pattern on his back.

Michael thinks to himself, "why am I in here looking at this man. I have a beautiful wife at home who loves me and is my best friend. Yet I feel so close to Jeffrey and intrigued by him. I have never felt this way before." Jeffrey notices that Michael looks distracted.

Jeffrey with hesitation in his voice says, "Are you alright? You got really quiet on me and we always have a lot to talk about."

"I'm ok Jeff, I just have a lot on my mind and I'm trying to place my thoughts in the right areas." They get out of the showers and stand in front of each other. Michael leans on the locker and drops his towel. Jeffrey reaches down to get the towel when Michael puts his hand on his shoulder to motion him back down. Jeffrey holds Michael's manhood and begins to please him. The pleasure was so intense and Michael enjoyed every moment of it. As the two men got lost in the passion of the moment, Michael's cell phone sends an alert that he had a message.

"Oh no, that's my wife. I better get going."

Jeffrey watches Michael rushing around in the locker room trying to gather himself as he dashes out the door. Michael arrives at the office and sees his wife standing by the entrance door. He looks flustered but pulls himself together to greet his wife with a hug. Michael says, "Hey honey, what are you doing here? I thought you had a meeting today." He starts to walk to his office and she's right behind him trying to catch up with him.

Tasha says with a slight attitude, "You don't remember that we were supposed to be having lunch today or were you so caught up at the gym working out that you forgot?"

Michael's mind flashes back to Jeffrey's lips touching his body.

He sighs and says, "Honey, once again I'm sorry I forgot about lunch. I was trying to burn off some stress. Let me check my emails and I will be ready in just a minute ok? Why don't you go out and talk to Shauntel while I answer my emails."

Tasha doesn't move very quickly but agrees to give him space and leaves his office to wait. Michael sits in his chair and gazes out the window trying to focus on work but all he can seem to think about is Jeffrey. He turns around and logs onto his computer and the first email he has is from Jeffrey. The subject line reads, "I can't stop thinking about you."

Michael's heart begins to beat fast and he feels extreme warmth infuse his body. He opens the email and starts to read. Jeffrey says, "What did you do to me? You captured a piece of my heart that I tried to bury deep in the pain of my previous failed relationships. I should feel bad about what happened and the terrible position I put you in but I don't. I wanna be near you and feel you in my arms again. I wanna look you in the face and see your eyes so intense with passion. And, most of all, I wanna touch you and please you again. I gotta go. Hope to see you soon. Jeff."

Michael's eyes begin to fill up with tears because of the act he committed. However, he feels a

freedom that he's never felt before.
Shauntel buzzes the intercom and
tells Michael his wife is still waiting.
Michael wipes his face, straightens
his tie and dashes a few drops of
cologne on before heading out the
door. Tasha and Michael go to the
local café down the street from
Michael's law office.

Michael looks distracted but
tries to keep a game face on to
avoid the questions. Tasha is very
perceptive and reads Michael like a
book. "So, Michael, where do you
want to go on vacation this year? I
was thinking maybe we can go to
Jamaica. We haven't been there
since our honeymoon. Remember
we had so much fun. That was
when you and I went jet skiing"

Michael nods his head and
motions for the waitress to take his
order. "Sure honey, whatever you
want."

Tasha stares Michael directly
in the face and says, "What the hell
is your problem? You have been
acting funny all day and now
you're barely talking to me and I
can't understand why?" Then,
Tasha's cell phone rings and she
says, "Do you mind if I answer this?

It's Paulette. She's in crisis with her
girlfriend and she needs me to talk
her off the ledge."
Michael nods his head "yes"
and she answers her phone.
"Hey, Girl, what's up? Yes,
I'm at lunch with my man. I'm sure
he won't mind if we hang out
tonight and catch a movie. Ok, I
will meet you downstairs at seven.
Alright, see you later." She hangs
up and begins to eat her salad that
the waitress just brought to the
table.

Michael checks his
blackberry. "Honey, I need to head
back to the office and get some
work done. I will most likely stay
there late since you're going out
with Paulie tonight. Then again, the
basketball comes on tonight too. I
think I will just work from home
instead."
Tasha says, "Sure that's fine
and you're ok with me going out
tonight, right? I knew the basketball
game is coming on and you be
consumed with that and your beer."
Michael laughs, "You're
probably right. Michael looks at his
phone again and then sends Jeff a

text that says come over to my place
at eight pm and don't be late.
He smiles and wipes his mouth
from a good meal. He gets up from
the table and kisses his wife on the
forehead and says, "Ok honey, I
will see you when you get home."

At the hospital, Jeffrey feels
the vibration of his phone and looks
to see the message from Michael
and becomes very excited about
spending time with his boo. "Well,
alright ladies it's on tonight! I get to
see my new man and hopefully we
will finish what we started."
One of the nurses laughed
and says, "You know you're wrong
because that man is married. You
should feel bad but I'm sure you
don't."
Jeffrey puts a sour look on his
face and replies with an attitude,
"Why you got to rain on my
rainbow parade. And if she was
taking care of her husband the way
I do he wouldn't be all into me now
would he? So, mind your business
and finish these charts so I can get
out of here." The nurses all look
and laugh at Jeffrey as he pretends
like he's on the catwalk.

Michael rushes out of the office and jumps on the train to get home faster. He showers and puts on some loose fitting basketball shorts and his favorite jersey.

Michael thinks to himself, "I can't wait to see Jeffrey again. I do feel guilty about what I'm doing but for some reason I can't help myself. He just gets me and will do anything to please me."

Tasha comes in and takes a shower as well and puts on her nightlife clothes and makeup. Michael looks at her and says in a joking manner, "Boo, looks like you're putting on a little weight and your face looks real shiny."

Tasha doesn't find Michael's humor very funny and grunts at him. "Maybe you should get me a membership at the gym with you and help me since you think I look like porky pig."

He pulls her close, "Honey, I was just joking. But you are glowing. Is it your makeup?"

She's kisses him and says, "Nope I don't have any foundation on. It's my natural beauty and don't you forget it." Michael tips her over and kisses her passionately. She giggles like a young teenager and runs toward the door. "I don't wanna be late to the movie. See you later and be ready to get it in tonight." Tasha says as she closes the door.

Michael thinks to himself and mumbles, "I sure will."

As opening tip begins on the basketball game, the doorbell rings and he runs to answer it. He checks under his arms and breathe to make sure he's still smells good. Michael opens the door and his breath catches in his throat as Jeffrey walks in. He stares at him and immediately catches himself and invites him in. Jeffrey looks around the penthouse and is amazed at all the art and pottery they have. He follows Michael into the family room and joins him on the couch. Michael does his best to play it cool but can't help but feel a little anxious. Deciding to break the ice he asks, "Why are you sitting so far away? You can come closer to me if you want." Jeffrey moves over quickly and smiles.

Would you like a beer Jeffrey or a glass of wine? I was just watching this game but right about now I could care less about it. All I want to do is kiss you". Jeffrey moves closer to Michael on the couch and says, No thank you. I don't feel like drinking tonight for some reason. I'm so glad you asked me to come over. All I've been thinking about is kissing you too."

Michael pulls Jeffrey's face close to him and their lips graze each other. Michael says with a soft voice, "So, why don't you? I'm not going to stop you." They begin to kiss passionately and caress each other. Jeffrey feels Michael begin to rise and takes advantage of the moment. He moved on top of Michael and started to grind on him.

Michael started to breath heavily and whispered, "Please do me like you did in the locker room."

Jeffrey slides down in between Michael's legs and starts to stroke him and kiss him. Michael's body begins to shake and he moans as Jeffrey rubbed his inner thighs. It seems like this moment lasted forever. Not knowing that it would end very quickly.

"Alright Paulie, I will see you tomorrow. Let me get in here and see what this man is doing," Tasha says as she places her keys in the door. She tries to balance her keys, bottle of merlot and her purse. She finally gets the door open and walks in. She hangs her keys on the key holder by the door and places her coat and purse on the coat hanger. It was like Tasha was walking on clouds not knowing that her husband, the love of her life was allowing a man to do things to him that she could only dream of. She walks into the living room and before she could say "I'm home" she sees Jeffrey's face buried in Michael's lap.

She shook uncontrollably and the bottle of wine fell to the floor and shattered into what seemed like a million pieces. Michael heard the bottle and saw his wife standing there shaking.
"Oh my God Tasha! I can explain. It's not what you think."
He jumped up and pulled his shorts up quickly. Jeffrey covered his mouth in fear and hid his face. Tasha screamed and ran towards the front door.

"Tasha, what a minute, let me explain." Michael says as he ran after her. Tasha was able to open the door and ran down the stairs and off into the street. She ran towards the train station and jumped the turnstile and caught the sub. Michael was right behind her but the doors slammed in his face. He tried to stop the train but was unsuccessful. She sat on the seat crying hysterically. She started to have trouble breathing. An elderly lady asks Tasha, "Are you ok honey? Did you get mugged out here? You shouldn't be alone this time of night." Tasha looks at the elderly lady with her eyes red and her makeup running down her face and says, "My whole world just ended."

"Hi Sweetie, my name is, Ms. Pearl. My grandson brought me this phone for emergencies and this looks like an emergency."

Tasha sat staring at the phone wondering who she could call and possibly tell them her husband had an affair with a man. She only knew one person in the city she could call and trust. She dialed Paulie's phone and began to sob again.

Paulie answered the phone sounding very puzzled because of the strange number. "Hello, who is this?" Tasha was so stricken with grief all she could do is cry.

Paulie says, "Stop playing on my phone! I'm about to hang up."

Pearl takes the phone and says, "Hello, I'm on the L train with a lady who is crying and she didn't know who to call. What's your name, dear?"

Tasha manages to breathe out, "Tasha," before falling into another fit of tears.

"She says her name is Tasha."

Paulie sat up from her bed and said, "What! Why is Tasha on the sub? Can you put her back on the phone please? Tasha! Can you hear me? What is going on? Where are you?"

Tasha gathered herself enough to say "Michael and Jeffrey, I can't believe he would do this to me. I thought he loved me and was faithful to me and we haven't even been here that long and he messes with a man. I'm so stupid, Paulie. How come I didn't see the signs? Did I cause him to be this way? I can't deal with this."

Paulie says, "Tasha, get off at
the next stop available and I will be
there to get her."

Ms. Pearl takes the phone
back and asks if the person on the
other line was still there.

Paulie says, "Yes I'm still
here. Can you have my friend get
off at the next stop which is
Madison Ave and I will be there as
soon as I can?"

Ms. Pearl says, "I sure will
and I will wait with your friend to
make sure she was safe." Paulie
thanks the lady and hung up. She
grabbed her sweatpants and hoodie
and jumped in a cab to avoid
waiting for the next train. She got to
Madison Ave within five minutes
and saw Tasha sitting on a park
bench with Ms. Pearl Paulie told the
cab to wait for her and she rushed
up the street to meet her distraught
friend. She looked at Tasha sitting
on the cold bench with no jacket on
shivering. She took her hoodie off
and wrapped it around her. Paulie
thanked Ms. Pearl for waiting with
her friend and offered to pay for a
cab so she could get home. Ms.
Pearl told the women she lived a
block away and would be fine with

walking. As Ms. Pearl, walks away,
she says "Be encouraged and God
be with you."

Paulie sat on the bench next
to Tasha and asked what happened.
Tasha couldn't form the words to
describe what she just witnessed.

All she could manage to say
is, "That bastard cheated on me
with a man."

Paulie didn't look surprised
at all and lifted Tasha off the bench.
She wiped the tears from her face
and said, "You will survive this
baby girl. I'm not gonna tell you I
told you so cause you never kick
someone when they're down but I
will say this, I know you love him
but he ain't worth it. Look at you?
Standing out here looking like the
world landed on your shoulders.
You are a successful
businesswoman with the drive and
determination to make it from the
projects to the palace. Don't allow
this man to crush your life and
cause you to lose yourself. You're
better than this."

Paulie put her arm around
Tasha and walked her to the cab.
Tasha took a deep sigh and said,
"What am I gonna do? I can't go

back there." Paulie told Tasha she
could stay with her and Jazz as long
as she wants. Tasha was relieved
but hesitates because Paulie's
apartment was a few floors down
from Tasha and Michael's
penthouse. But, she agreed and
begged Paulie to keep Michael
away from her. Paulie asked the cab
driver to park in the back of the
apartment complex to ensure they
wouldn't see Michael.

In the penthouse Jeffrey sat
on the couch with his head between
his legs. Jeffrey waited for Michael
to come back so the penthouse
doors wouldn't be open.
Michael walked in and began
to cry and said, "I can't believe this.
I hurt my best friend and I don't
know if she will ever forgive me."
Jeffrey walks towards Michael and
started to rub his back. Michael
wanted to push Jeffrey away but
felt so comfortable with him there.
Jeffrey wanted to tell Michael
everything would be ok and that
Tasha would come home so they
could talk but he believed those
words wouldn't make him feel
better.

Michael asked, "Jeffrey, can you leave so I could sort things out. I will call you as soon as I find my wife." Jeffrey understood and left. Michael went to the kitchen and grabbed the broom and mop to clean up the pieces of broken glass and wine.

Michael yells, "Tasha, please come home! The silence is killing me and the torture of not knowing where you are his driving me crazy!"

After he cleaned up everything and took a shower, he decided to go downstairs to Paulie's apartment and ask her if she had heard or seen his wife. He rang the intercom and Paulie knew exactly who it was. Tasha was resting in the spare bedroom.

Paulie answered the intercom by saying, "Who is this?"

Michael leaned against her door and said, "It's Michael, Tasha's husband. Is she there or have you heard from her?"

Paulie frowned her face behind the door and says, "Nah, I haven't seen her since the movie. She came home right after the movie. Weren't you there when she got home? Lord, please forgive me for lying." She looked at Michael through the peephole as he paced up and door the hallway. He sat there for another minute and then walked away. Paulie walked away from the door and went to the spare bedroom where Tasha was lying down to see if she needed anything but she was asleep. Jazz walked up behind Paulie and whispered,

"Baby, is she ok? She looks so drained and I'm worried about her."

Paulie held Jazz's hand and they went to the bedroom to talk in private. They held each other on the bed and Paulie says, "Honey, I really don't know. Her whole world just blew up in her face and she doesn't know how to handle it. I can't imagine how I would deal with something like this. I know we haven't known Tasha that long but, she reached out to me and I can't watch her go through this alone. Do you have a problem with her staying with us?"

Jazz reluctantly says, "I guess so. This is so crazy. I don't mean to sound insensitive but, I hope she can get herself together and figure out where she's gonna go in a few days." Paulie stops holding Jazz and gives her the most chilling stare.

"Jazz, how could you say something like that? This woman just found out her husband has betrayed her and not just with a woman but a man. She needs sisterly support and if you can't be that then maybe you should go back to your apartment and stay there for a minute. I'm so not feeling you right now. I never thought you could be this insensitive and selfish. Matter of fact, it's not a maybe you should go back to your place, I want you to leave. We need some space to reevaluate our relationship."

Jazz began to cry and angrily says, "Are you serious Paulie? You're really going to ask me to leave because of how I feel? I guess I really didn't know you like that and from what I'm seeing this isn't what I signed up for. I will be out in the morning." Jazz grabbed the blankets off the bed and went to sleep on the couch. Paulie gets up and slams the bedroom door as Jazz walks away.

The next morning, Tasha waits for Michael to leave for work and she goes upstairs to gather her clothes and special possessions that she cherished the most. As she stood in the doorway of the family room, she felt a nauseous feeling come over her. She ran to the bathroom and began to vomit. Tasha pulled herself off the floor and told herself not to cry. She picked up her clothes and box and closed the door. As she settled into Paulie's spare room, she looked at the pictures in her box. One picture was from their college senior dance and the others were from their wedding. Tasha begins to talk out loud, "What did I do so wrong for this to happen to me? I love Michael with all of my heart and soul and just don't understand how he's going to cheat on me. Could I have missed the signs that Michael was on the DL all the time?"

Tasha shakes her head and turns on her cell phone only to have fifteen voicemails from Michael and two from her parents asking why Michael was looking for her. She also had twenty-five text messages from Michael begging her to come home and to give him a chance to explain. She deleted all of the voicemails and text messages.

Tasha calls her parents and says, "Hi mommy. How are you? No, I'm not ok. I really need to come home for awhile. I'm separating from Michael. I really can't explain everything to you right now. I will be there in a few weeks. I have some clients I am working with and I just can't leave them now. So, I am staying with a good friend. Please don't worry about me. I will make it through this situation. I will call later tonight ok?" Tasha hangs up and starts to cry in frustration. Paulie comes home and hears Tasha crying.

"Hey, Tasha, you ok? Did Michael call you or did you see him? You know Jazz moved out, right? She mad because I won't let her have her way and she needs to grow up. This is why I stayed single for so long. Did you want anything to eat? I'm sure you don't feel like going out anywhere and I don't cook."

They both laugh and Tasha smiles and says, "You know this is the first time I have smiled in what seems like forever. Thank you so much for opening your home to me and I will be out of your hair in a week or two if that's ok. I have to finish these projects with my clients before I leave to go home to my parents. I hate to go back there but I can't be in this city right now. I need to clear my head. I really like it here but I just don't want to run into Michael."

Paulie replies, "Yeah, I totally understand that. Well, my door is always open to you. You don't have to rush to leave but if being here is a constant reminder of Michael maybe you should go back home for awhile."

Two weeks went by and Tasha decided to pick up the pieces of her life. She contacted an attorney and had him draw up the divorce papers. She sat at Paulie's table looking at the papers and started to cry. Paulie came in and rubbed her back. All of a sudden, she felt so sick, she ran to the bathroom to vomit. Tasha washes her face and brushed her teeth. "Girl, I don't know why I can't keep anything down lately. Smells make me sick and certain food has me running to the restroom."

"Are you ok?" Paulie says appearing in the bathroom doorway

"I think so." Tasha says drying her mouth. "I must have picked up a bug from work."

Paulie started thinking and says, "Maybe you should take a pregnancy test."
Tasha looked in the mirror and her mind went back to Michael saying she looked like she was gaining weight and she was glowing. Paulie reaches under the counter and takes out a test for Tasha.

"Why the hell do you have pregnancy tests under your sink?" Tasha asks incredulously.

Paulie laughs, "I used to make my girlfriend take the test after we had sex to see if I was able to get her pregnant."

Tasha fell out laughing and then she got silent thinking about what happens if she is pregnant. She took the test and waited for the results. When the stick turned a bright blue, her heart dropped and she says to Paulie, "Whelp, looks like you're going to be a godfather." Tasha laughs at her own joke and then her smile turns into fear and confusion.

Paulie opened the door and Tasha stood in front of her crying. They embraced, "What are you going to do?" Paulette asked Tasha. Tasha responded, "I'm going to leave these divorce papers, my rings, and this test on his table and move on with my life." Paulie said, "Good for you and you know I will always be here for you and the baby." Tasha thanked her and went upstairs before Michael arrived home from work. She looked around the apartment one more time and placed the test, papers and rings on the kitchen table. She whispered a pray and said good bye.

Michael and Jeffrey arrive back to the penthouse and Michael notices a yellow envelope on the table that wasn't there before he left from work. He picks up the envelope and notices it is addressed to him and the handwriting is Tasha's. He sits down and opens the envelope and pours everything inside on the table. Michael picks up the wedding rings and sees the signed divorce papers. His heart begins to beat fast and sweat begins to pour from his head. Then, Michael sees the positive pregnancy test. He stares at the test and says, "Oh my God! Tasha is pregnant! This can't be. She's having my baby." He sees another separate piece of paper and starts to read it.

"Michael, I never thought our lives would take such a dramatic turn. And, I thought our love would last forever. I don't understand how we got here. I thought you could talk to me about everything. And to have to betray me with a man is so unforgivable. I need to move on and obviously you already have. Don't worry about me. I will be just fine. I will always love you but, I can't live this way. I wish you the best. ~ Tasha"

Michael pushed the table over and screamed to the top of his lungs as he falls to the floor. Jeffrey ran into the dining room to see the table pushed over and Michael lying on the floor. Jeffrey lies next to Michael and says, "Baby, are you alright? What is going on?" Jeffrey

sees the divorce papers on the
ground and the pregnancy test
across the room. He mouth opens
wide in shock of what he's just
witnessed. Michael tries to gather
himself but can't seem to find the
strength to get off the floor.

"Jeff, I can't believe she's having my
baby and I'm not here for her. I
have to find her someway. I can't let
her do this alone. I'm so confused.
This is so unbelievable.

Chapter Seven

After searching for almost a year and not being able to find Tasha he gave up and decided to move on with Jeffrey. Michael arrived home before Jeffrey and decided to work on some papers in his study. As he searched through some boxes of files, he came across a dusty box sitting in the corner of the room. He picks the box up and places it on his desk. He begins to walk away but something from the box draws him in and he decides to sit and look through the belongings.

Michael picks up the picture of him and Tasha on his wedding day. He begins to reminisce on what was the happiest day of his life. As they danced the night away and he holds Tasha tight in his arms, he whispers in her ear, "I will never let you go. I love you baby and one day we will watch our children on their wedding days feel the same happiness I feel at this moment."

Echoes of the song "I Will Love You Always," by Atlantic star filled the air and Michael kissed Tasha passionately. Michael continued to look at all the wonderful memories stuffed in this little box. The tears began to flow as he read an anniversary card Tasha gave him a few years ago. The words "I will love you forever" pierced his heart like a dagger. Michael held the picture of Tasha close to his heart and smelled the perfumed scented letters she wrote him when they first started dating. At the bottom of the box was the positive pregnancy test and he couldn't help but to feel guilty. As he hears the front door open, Michael wiped his face, kisses the picture and gently places the items back in the box.

"Hey, Babe, I'm home." Jeffrey breezes in the door. "Wow, I had a long day at the hospital. I'm gonna get dinner started in a minute. How was your day?" Jeffrey says kissing Michael before walking into the bedroom to change his clothes.

Michael walks into the living room and sits on the couch. He replies, "Fine, Jeff. I'm tired, ok."

Noticing the tone of Michael's voice, Jeffrey peeks into the living room before going into the kitchen. Jeffrey feels like something is bothering Michael besides being tired. Michael flips through the channels on the television but, his mind is wondering if Tasha is ok. Jeffrey continues to talk to Michael and Michael continues to ignore him.

After a few minutes of the silence, Jeffrey puts the food in the oven and enters the living room for some quality time with Michael thinking that maybe this will mellow his mood. He sits close to Michael on the couch and Michael moves over to create space between him and Jeffrey.

"Baby what's wrong? Why are you acting so distant toward me?" Jeffrey asks in a small voice.

Michael stands up and goes to the kitchen to get a snack. He comes back and sits on the love seat instead of the couch with Jeffrey.

Michael takes a deep breath and says, "I don't know what's wrong with me. It's not you Jeff. I guess I'm just missing her." At first Jeffrey looks a little puzzled and then realizes he's talking about his ex-wife Tasha. Jeffrey's face sinks low and he starts to become irritated with the conversation. Michael continues to talk and says, "I really hurt her and I never had a chance to make things right. Tasha was pregnant with my baby. I don't know what would have happened."

Jeffrey stands up and kneels in front of Michael. He grabs Michael's hands and says with a stern voice, "Honey, if she was pressed about you she would have reached out to you by now. And, if she had your baby you would've got served with custody and child support papers. Chile, please, she left without a trace almost a year ago and she ain't worried about you. So, why can't you just be happy with me?"

Michael pulls his hands away from Jeffrey and walks away. Michael heads toward his bedroom and changed into his workout clothes. Michael heads towards the door and angrily says, "I'm going to work out. I need some alone time. I won't be long." Jeffrey watches the door slam in his face as Michael leaves.

Chapter Eight

Tasha arrived back into Chicago and found a small house outside of the city. "Tasha, where do you want to put these boxes at?" Paulie says as she struggles to balance the boxes.

Tasha walks into the front door holding a beautiful baby boy in her arms and says, "You can put them in Mitch's room. Did you hear that, Buddy? You have your own room. And you have me and Aunt Paulie to take care of you."

Tasha lays the baby in his car seat and begins to browse through a couple of boxes next to her. She opens a box and stares at a photo of Michael and starts to feel a cold sensation overtake her body. Tasha whispers to God, "What did I do so wrong to make my life this way? How can I ever trust another man again?" She looks toward the ceiling and begins to weep.

Paulie walks into the room and sits next to Tasha. She pulls Tasha toward her to hold her. Paulie wipes the tears from her face. She says in a gentle voice, "Tasha, I know it still hurts but you will heal

from this. I know today would have
been your wedding anniversary.
Why don't we take Mitch out to the
park? I'm sure you could both
could use a breath of fresh air."

Paulie leads Tasha out of the
house with Mitch placed in his
stroller. They walk to the local park
down the street from their home.
"See Tasha, I told you being outside
would do you a world of good."
They walk the trail that leads them
into another park a few blocks
away.

On the other side of town,
Michael arrives at the crowded
fitness center and decides to take a
run in the park instead. As Michael
runs to clear his mind, flashes of
Tasha and their life together fill his
mind. He runs faster in the hopes of
the memories fading away. Michael
runs past two people pushing a
stroller. He slowed down and
looked back thinking one of the
people was Tasha.

Tasha sees a gentleman run by
but doesn't see his face, but the
smell of Burberry cologne makes
her stop in her tracks. She would
know the scent anywhere because it
was the cologne she bought Michael

on their first anniversary. He would
ask for that cologne on every
holiday. She took a deep breath and
kept walking.

Suddenly, Tasha slowly turns
around to see a man standing in the
distance on the running path. Tasha
then looks at Paulette and says,
"No, it can't be. Let's keep going. I
really can't do this."

Michael runs back to speak to
her. "Tasha, is it really you?"
Michael asks with a smile on his
face. "Wow, you look great. It's
been so long since I've seen you,
Wow."

Tasha looks at him with a frown
and says, "Yeah, it's been a year. I
gotta go. Take care."

Michael is so amazed with her
beauty he almost lets her walk
away without noticing Tasha
pushing a stroller. He glances inside
and sees a little boy who looks
identical to Michael as a small child.

Michael immediately stops her
and says, "Wait a minute! Is this my
son? How could you hide him from
me?"

"Michael, you chose this life for
yourself and if you weren't busy
playing boyfriend you would have

made more of an effort to fight for our marriage." Tasha's eyes held such hatred that Michael took a step back. "You lied to me and I trusted you. You were my best friend and you betrayed me. Now, you wanna care because we have a son? I did the both of you a favor by not telling you so our baby wouldn't grow up confused. Don't bother, ok. We are doing just fine without you," Tasha says as she walks away.

Michael attempts to stop her and Paulie steps in front of him to allow Tasha and the baby to leave. Paulie extends her arms and says, "Mike, dude you need to fall back and give her some space. It's been a year and both of you are emotional. Let me talk to her and I will get at you later. I know where you work and how to contact you."

Michael agreed and walked away. He walks around the park until it is dark thinking about Tasha and his son. He says to himself, "I can't believe I have a son. I don't even know his name. He looks just like me. I missed a year of his life. I would never want my children to grow up without a father. I wasn't there for Tasha when she needed me the most. I have been so selfish."

Michael walks back home and is greeted at the door by Jeffrey. Jeffrey puts his arms around Michael and say, "Baby, I am so sorry about what I said to you. I don't understand how you feel and I was insensitive to say all those hateful things about Tasha and her supposed baby."

Michael stands with a blank look on his face. He holds his arms to the sides of his body.

Michael looks Jeffrey in the eyes and said the words Jeffrey dreaded to hear since they became a couple. "I saw Tasha and I have a son."

Jeffrey's mouth drops opens and his eyes as wide as saucers. Michael goes to the wine cabinet in the kitchen. Michael stands there looking at the bottle and says, "For a whole year she hid him from me! He looks just like me when I was a kid. I would never leave my son without a father!" Out of frustration, he throws the bottle at the kitchen wall.

Michael screams, "Dammit! I need to find her and my son. I want my son in my life."

Jeffrey stands off in the distance watching Michael have this breakdown. He becomes very angry and says, "Well, what you gonna do, Honey? This bitch knows she's wrong and needs to pay for this! We gonna fight and get your son here with us."

Michael gets directly in Jeffrey's face and puts his finger out as if he's scolding him and responds, "Don't you dare insult my wife and son like that!"

Jeffrey is so shocked from Michael's reaction that he walks to the bedroom and screams, "She's not your wife anymore!"

Chapter Nine

Tasha and Paulie arrive home and try to gather themselves after the awkward encounter with Michael. Mitchell has fallen asleep on the way home so Tasha takes him out the stroller and lays him down in his room. Paulie goes to the kitchen to make a sandwich and Tasha joins her to talk. Tasha looks as if her world has ended again.

"Paulie, what am I gonna do?" Paulette pushes the plate away and says, "We both knew this day would come. And yes, the pain and hurt has resurfaced but, you need to be realistic with yourself. You still love him and I believe he still loves you. Love doesn't change situations, circumstances do. Michael has a piece of your heart and Mitchell is a reminder of your love for each other. He was conceived in love. Yes, the lies and deceit make it hard to believe but he was. Maybe it's time you break your silence and talk to him. He owes you an explanation and apology. And, he deserves a chance to get to know his son."

Tasha laughs, "When did you become so wise? You sound like a fortune cookie."

Paulie giggles as well and stands up to take a bow. "Tasha, if you had been through half of what I've been through, you would've lost your mind. I'm single and ready to mingle then I meet a woman who I think I can have some adult fun with and she becomes clingy. Then, I find myself hiding and trying to get away from her. And, for some dumb reason people think you and I are together. I have to keep explaining to them that you can have a gay roommate and not be sleeping with them."

Tasha gets up from the table and agrees that you can be cool with someone and not be intimate with them. They both flop down on the couch to watch a movie. "Paulie, you are my best friend and I know you would never try anything because you look at me as a sister."

Paulie hugs Tasha and says, "You're absolutely right. We are sisters and that's why I can tell you the truth even when you don't wanna hear it. So stop being so stubborn and set a time to meet

Mike for lunch. Or would you like
me to be the go between so you
don't have to deal with him?"

Tasha sighs, "Yes, please contact
him and tell him we can meet for
lunch Friday at the café around the
corner from his job."

Paulie looked strange at Tasha
and asked, "Why Friday?"

Tasha stands up and prances
around the room like a supermodel,
"I need to get my hair done, nails
and feet done, and Mitchell needs a
haircut and we both need new
outfits. We can't meet my baby
daddy all busted!"

Paulie falls off the couch
laughing and says, "Well alright,
Tasha! Get it girl! I will call his
office tomorrow morning and let
him know the ground rules." They
both laugh at each other and start
the movie.

Chapter Ten

Michael sat in his office looking out the window and all he could think about for the past two days was Tasha and his son. Michael's secretary informs him that he has a visitor. Michael was intrigued on who it could be. He was hoping it was Tasha but then again the secretary would have said it was his ex wife. His door opens and Paulie walks in.

"Paulie, please have a seat. I'm so glad you're here I was wondering if…"

"Listen Michael, I need to do the talking and you do the listening." Paulette cuts him off. "First of all, I still don't like you and I always thought you were on the down low but, I gave you the benefit of the doubt. So, your behavior doesn't surprise me. But, I'm not here to tell you how much of a screw up you are." Paulie decides to take a seat.

"I'm here to help you make the wrong right for your sake. Tasha has agreed to see you Friday and bring Mitchell with her."

Michael's smile is so big and he pokes his chest out. "My son's name is Mitchell? Wow, Tasha actually gave him the name we talked about back in the day. I didn't want him named Michael Jr. I wanted to give him a powerful name and we both said Mitchell Alexander. Is that his whole name, Paulie?"

Paulie smirked and shook her head "yes." Michael lies back in his chair and kicks his feet up on his desk. Paulie chimes in and says, "You need to focus ok? She will meet you at the local café downstairs. Do not, and I mean do not tell or bring Jeffrey with you. If you have any hopes of having a relationship with your son and his mother you need to keep that queen as far away from them as possible. Don't bring her flowers or gifts for Mitchell. All that will do is make her believe you're trying to buy their affection and love. And lastly, don't say anything stupid."

"I can do that," Michael says seriously.

Paulie stood up to leave and Michael went to hug her. She straight armed him in the chest and said, "Don't even try that with me. I'm not your friend. I'm Tasha's

best friend and I want what's best
for her and Mitchell. Don't mess
this up."

After Paulie left and Michael
couldn't help but jump up and
down with excitement about his
lunch date. Michael wanted to tell
Jeffrey but knew if he breathed a
word of this it could destroy his
chances with Tasha. So, he held
onto the secret.

Friday morning, Michael pulled
out his best suit and the tie and
shirt set Tasha bought him. He
shaved his head and polished his
shoes. Jeffrey noticed how Michael
was taking his time with getting
dressed and being very particular.
He looked like a million bucks.

Jeffrey pulled Michael by his suit
jacket before he could walk out the
door and said, "Damn, you look
good. Can you be a little late to
work today so you can take care of
me?"

Michael fixed his jacket and
replied, "No, I need to focus today
and I don't want or need anything
to distract me. I have a very
important meeting today. I will call

you when I get home. Have a good
day." He opened the door and left.

"I love you too," Jeffrey
murmured under his breath.
Michael looked at his watch and
saw it was 11:45am. "Yes, it's
almost twelve o' clock. I get to see
my son."

Michael went downstairs to
make   reservations for two. "May I
also have a booster seat?" he smiled
as they gave him the booster seat.

He sat at the table with a glass of
water and stared at the door.
Michael thought to himself, "What
if she doesn't show up? I hope
Mitchell doesn't cry when he sees
me. I have waited for this moment
and I need to keep a calm head."
Noon Tasha walks in holding
Mitchell.

Michael stood up to greet Tasha
with a kiss and she declined. He
wanted to pick Mitchell up and
squeeze him tight but he didn't
want to frighten him on the first
meeting. Michael couldn't help but
to show his excitement about his
family being together. He went to
touch Tasha's hand and she
abruptly stopped him.

"Michael, please. This isn't about us it's about Mitchell. Tasha holds Mitchell close to her and says, "Michael, this is Mitchell Alexander Davis. Would you like to hold him?"
Michael beamed with pride as he took the little hand into his larger one. He didn't want to let his son go. "Tasha, yes I would love to hold him. He's amazing. You named him Mitchell Alexander. This is such a happy day. I wish I would have been there when he was born. But, I can't blame you no matter how much I want to be mad at you I can't." He looked at Tasha for a moment and was drunk in her beauty. How could he have let things get so bad? When she didn't say anything he continued.

"Honey, I'm sorry for how things went down. I should have been honest with you about my past and my struggle. That wasn't fair to you to keep that from you. If you give me a chance I will explain everything. But, I really wanna be in Mitchell's life." Michael wasn't usually known for speaking with such relaxed speed, but in this situation he figured it was best that

he let go and open his heart. "I
know I can't make up for the past
year I missed but, I'm willing to do
what it takes to make that happen.
Just tell me what you want."

Tasha looked at Michael and
knew he was serious. Her heart
melted a little but she couldn't get
over what he had done to her. The
male waiter came to the table to
take their order. He was tall and
slender and had a body shaped like
a woman. The waiter was very
feminine and couldn't help but to
try and flirt with Michael. Tasha
saw it first hand and got very upset.

"Michael, is this how you do
things? You gonna really flirt with
this fag in front of me and your
son?" Michael couldn't believe
Tasha had talked to him like that.
Throwing his napkin on his plate he
retaliates, "Now you wait a damn
minute, Tasha. You're not going to
disrespect me in front of my son."

Tasha looks like she could reach
over the table and smack Michael
right in the face and remembered he
was holding Mitchell. She reaches
over and takes the baby out of his
arms. "Disrespect you! Are you
serious? Don't you dare try to act

like you're offended because I called that thing a faggot? And, you act like what he did was ok. What if we were still married, would you have allowed that to happen? And, he did it in front of our son. Furthermore, if anyone should be offended it would be Mitchell to see that display of filth in his face. You have a lot to learn about children and how to raise them. I don't know if you ready for this Michael. You still have a lot of growing up to do and need to figure out what's important to you. Is your "man" more important than a relationship with your son? You can't have both and I won't allow my son to be confused by you. This meeting is over. I can't believe you gonna look at that dude in front of me like I'm chopped liver. I will call you tomorrow and let you know when you can see Mitchell again. I can't be around you right now. Goodbye."

Michael tries to stop her but it was too late. He sat at the table with his head down. In his mind he says, "I did it again. Paulie warned me not to do anything stupid and I did. I just can't win. But, she did say

she would call me tomorrow. So, I
guess that means she will try to
give me a chance."

Tasha is so frustrated with
Michael and his attitude she forgets
her purse on the table and has to go
back to the restaurant all the while
hoping Michael has left already.

Entering the café, she is happy to
see that Michael has indeed left.
The only problem now is that her
purse is gone. "I hope Michael
didn't take my purse," she inwardly
groans.

"Are you looking for a small
purse?" a deep voice says as Tasha
walks to the bar.

Turning around, Tasha sees a
handsome chocolate man. "Yes I
am. Do you know where it is?"
Tasha asks.

"I gave it to the bartender. They
tried to seat me at the table where I
found it. I told the waiter who was
too friendly to seat me at the bar
where I have room."

They both laugh and for the first
time all day Tasha genuinely smiles.
The gentleman smiles back and
said, "My name is, William, nice to
meet you and the little guy.

Tasha is hesitant but deciding that he looks harmless enough introduces herself, "My name is Tasha and this is my son, Mitch. Nice to meet you, William."

William smiles and invites the two of them to eat lunch with him. Tasha said, "That's very nice of you but, I really need to go. I'm dealing with a lot and don't think I will be good company."

William says, "I understand and hope I can get a rain check. I feel silly asking you out like this. Believe it or not this is my first time doing this. Can I give you my card and maybe when things settle for you, you could call me sometime?" William reaches in his briefcase and hands Tasha his card. She looks at the card and sees his full name and title, Dr. William H. Hines, DDS.

Impressed Tasha says, "Maybe I will look you up when I need a fill." They both laugh and she starts to walk away.

William said to her as she's leaving, "Tasha, by the way you look beautiful."

Tasha can't help but blush. Waving she pushes through the revolving door.

Chapter Eleven

Michael has the hardest time concentrating after spending time with Tasha and Mitchell. He was mad at himself and Tasha for making him seem like he had a problem.

Instead of going to work early he decided to go to the nightclub Paulie owned to talk to her and see if Tasha had said anything. The club wasn't open yet so she was the only one there.

"Paulie, I messed up. She hates me and walked out on me. What am I gonna do? She said she will call me tomorrow to arrange a time to spend with Mitchell but I need time with her too."

Paulie stepped off the ladder and said, "Why do you need time with her? Don't you have a man? And isn't that the life you chose for yourself?"

He helps her lift a box and says, "Yes, Jeff and I are still together but, I don't know what I want anymore. I miss Tasha and I want my son in my life. But I do love Jeff. She made it clear I can't have both."

Paulie continued to work and Michael followed her around the club. Paulie really didn't want to talk to Michael but she couldn't help asking, "What's more important to you? Is having a man in your life more important than having your son and wife back?"

Michael sits on a bar stool and places his hands on his head. He replies, "I want a relationship with my son. Outside of that, I don't know right now. You think Tasha is gonna call me tomorrow? Can I have her number to call her? Where does she live?"

Paulie stops filling the ice machine and said to Michael, "Now, you are asking too many questions and I need to get ready for tonight. If she says she will call you tomorrow then let her call you. Just be patient and make things better this time around."

Realizing that he is going to get anything else out of Paulette, Michael leaves just as frustrated as he was when he entered.

Just as Paulie was about to lock up, a slender, light skin woman opens the door. "Are you still looking for another bartender? I saw the help wanted sign posted on the window." Paulie invited the woman in. She watched her walk in to check her out from behind.

The woman said, "Where are my manners? My name is Leslie but everyone calls me Tiger. I know it's a weird name but it's because of the color of my eyes and skin. My dad said when I was born I was brown like a tiger with these greenish hazel eyes."

Paulie said, "Let me get a closer look of your eyes." She got close to Leslie's face and looked her straight in the eyes. Their eyes locked on each other and Leslie took a deep exhale.

Leslie said, "Wow, ok. That's never happened before. I'm sorry for staring at you."

Paulie shook her head and said, "If you allow yourself to get lost in someone's eyes it can happen again. Oh, and my name is Paulette but all my friends call me, Paulie. There's no story behind my name but, I definitely like your story, Tiger." Paulie takes a moment to collect herself.

"So, what experience do you have in bartending and does working in a gay bar bother you?"

Leslie says while laughing, "Does it look like I'm uncomfortable?"

Paulie sits next to her on a bar stool and answers, "No, not at all. I think you will fit right in here."

Leslie gives Paulie her resume and references. Paulie looks over the papers and sees that she is highly recommended from her last job in New York.

Paulie said, "I think I can try you out for a month and see how you work here. Would that be ok? And also what made you leave New York?" Leslie smiled and responded, "Yes that will be great. I left New York because I needed a change. I've lived there all my life and as big as New York is, it seemed like I knew everyone there. Plus, I needed to have some fun. I was in a long term relationship with my ex-girlfriend and she wanted more than what I was ready to give her. I'm not trying to get married and have any kids. I wanna enjoy my mate and live life to the fullest."

Paulie says, "Oh yeah we're going to get along really well. Come back tonight and I will show you the ropes. You get paid fifteen dollars an hour plus tips to start off. If you can make it past the first month, we can discuss getting more money. Sound good to you?"

Leslie stands up and says, "Yes, it sounds great and I will be back tonight to see how you do it." Leslie winks as she walked away.

Paulie smiles showing her dimples in her cheeks and walked Leslie to the door to let her out. Paulie couldn't wait to get home to tell Tasha that she had met someone today. Paulie was greeted at the door by Mitchell rolling around in his walker. His face lights up and he reaches for her to pick him up.

She swung him around and said, "Hey buddy!"

She puts him back in the walker and heads to the kitchen where Tasha is standing.

"Tasha, do I have something to tell you. I met someone at the bar that I hired and she's fine!"

Tasha looks surprised and says, "Oh for real? Well, my lunch with

Michael was a bust but, my day got better afterward. I left my purse on the table and a nice gentleman who by the way is a dentist found it and returned it to me. He asked me and Mitchell to have lunch with him. But, I'm not ready for that especially with Michael popping up in the picture. He did however give me his card. So, maybe I will call him someday."

Paulie looks Tasha up and down and replies, "Well look at you. This day turned out better than you thought. I know what happened at the lunch. Michael came over and told me everything. He looked so pitiful but I was nice and didn't laugh in his face. You gonna call that man tomorrow?"

Tasha puts a smirk on her face and her hands on her hips. "Paulie, as bad as I don't want too, I'm gonna call him tonight. He pissed me off but I at least wanna give him a chance to talk to me and say goodnight to Mitchell. I'm gonna be the bigger person this time around."

Paulie says, "Well, good for you and after you finish your call I wanna tell you all about Tiger."

"Tiger, Paulie? Oh Lord this is
gonna be a mess."

Chapter Twelve

Tasha walks into her bedroom to call Michael. She grabs her phone and calls his cell phone. Michael picks up on the first ring. "Hello, this is, Michael Davis."

Tasha says, "Hello Michael, its Tasha. I know I said I would call you tomorrow but I thought maybe we can talk tonight if you're not busy."

Michael steps out on the patio and closes the door for privacy. Jeffrey looks out the window thinking his actions are strange but decided to give him the space he obviously wanted.

"I'm free to talk now. I'm really sorry about this afternoon. I didn't want our first lunch date to end that way. Are you ok?"

Tasha says, "I'm fine and it wasn't a date Mike. We aren't dating or married anymore. I didn't call to talk about us but to find out what you're plans are for this weekend. I thought maybe you would like to go to the carnival with us? Not as a couple but as two parents sharing the day with their son."

"Yes I would love to go," Michael responds excitedly. Where can I meet you and what time? I'm so excited.

Tasha tells Michael to meet her at the carnival by the front gate. Michael agrees and Tasha asks, "Would you like to speak to Mitchell?"

Michael is so happy his cheeks begin to hurt from smiling "Thank you. Tasha, I would love to speak to him."

"Hey, Buddy, it's your da... I mean Mr. Mike." He catches himself before saying the word "dad."

"It was nice meeting you today and I pray we get to spend more time together. Sleep tight, Son."

Mitchell starts pressing the buttons and Michael couldn't help but to laugh. Tasha takes the phone back and says, "Mike, I'm here."

"Tasha, thank you again for letting me talk with Mitchell. Could I talk to him and you tomorrow?"

Tasha answers, "Yes" after a moment of silence. "Well, goodnight, Mike."

Before she can hang up, Michael replies, "It is now, Honey. Goodnight, talk to you tomorrow." Michael couldn't sleep with the anticipation of meeting Tasha and Mitchell at the carnival on Saturday. He lies in bed and feels Jeffrey pushing himself closer to Michael hoping he can make love to him.

Jeffrey whispers, "Baby, you've been so quiet these past two days. Anything going on you want to talk about? Matter of fact, let's not talk. How about I make your toes curl tonight?"

Michael doesn't want to have sex with him but he knows if he doesn't it will be hard to get away from him tomorrow to go to the carnival with Tasha and Mitchell. "Sure, Boo, I would like for you to make my toes curl. And, yes, everything is ok." He hopes that he sounds convincing. "Oh, by the way, I am working on a case that needs my special attention and I will be going into the office in the morning and won't be back until late. Hope you don't mind that. Plus, you didn't plan anything for us this weekend anyway."

Jeffrey jumps on top of Michael and says, "Of course I understand you have to go into work. I know when you are focused on something you won't stop until you get the best results. That's the reason why my ex is in jail and I got all my money back. I can't express to you how much you mean to me. I love you, boo." Jeffrey begins to grind Michael and they begin to make love.

After they finish, Michael rolls out of bed and takes a shower. In his mind he thinks about Tasha and Mitchell.

"I really wanna call her but I know it's too late. I can't stop thinking about her and my baby." Michael dries off and puts his shorts on. As he tiptoes across the room, he hears Jeffrey snoring and slides in bed.

In the morning, Michael smells fresh coffee and bacon cooking. He smiles and lays there as Jeffrey comes into the bedroom with a tray of food, coffee and fresh fruit. Jeffrey places the tray on the bed and says, "I figure you will need your strength for today since you usually don't work on Saturdays.

I'm going to catch up with my girls and do a little shopping. So, enjoy your food and I will see you later. Text me when you get a free moment."

Jeffrey leans over and kisses Michael and departs to have a fun day. Michael smiles and eats all of the treats Jeffrey prepared for him. After he finishes, he takes another shower and puts on his brand new jeans and polo shirt. He grabs the box of new air Jordan sneakers out the closet and a black fitted cap to cover his head. He gets his keys and runs out to catch the subway downtown to the carnival.

He waits patiently by the front entrance for Tasha and Mitchell. "The waiting for Tasha is so awful. I guess some things never change." He laughs to himself and then sees her from a distance pushing the stroller.

As she approaches the gate, Michael steps to Tasha and extends his arms for a hug. Tasha gives in and hugs him. She breathes deeply and for the first time she felt her heartbeat again. Michael holds her close and says, "I missed you so much."

Suddenly, Tasha pulls away and clears her throat. She utters, "I think we should go in."

Michael agrees and takes his wallet out to pay for their admission into the carnival. The family walks around the carnival looking at the rides and playing the games together. Then, Michael sees the merry-go-round and says, "Can we ride this together? I would like to take a few pictures if that's ok with you."

Tasha shakes her head "yes" and they give the attendant the tickets to enter the ride. Michael helps Tasha onto the porcelain horse as she held their baby close. He stood by her side as the ride took off. Michael looks at Tasha and Mitchell with such a feeling of hope. He takes out his camera and starts taking pictures. Michael and Tasha make silly faces in the camera and laugh together like old times. As the ride starts to slow down, Michael starts to get a little down.

"Michael, what's wrong? We were having fun and all of a sudden you get sad," Tasha notices his shift in mood.

Michael holds Mitchell's hand and says, "I don't want this day to end. There are so many things I need and want to say to you."

Just as Michael starts to share his feelings they hear someone yelling his name. Looking up they see Jeffrey and his group of friends standing at the exit of the merry-go-round. Michael's heart starts to beat fast knowing that he's caught in a big lie. Michael helps Tasha off the ride and puts Mitchell in his stroller. Jeffrey boils with anger when he hears his friends laugh at him.

"For real Michael, you gonna do this to me? Like really, did you need to lie to me for this stank, Bitch?"

Tasha's face turns red and she starts to step in Jeffrey's face.

Michael jumps in between them and says, "who you calling a bitch Jeffrey? This doesn't have anything to do with Tasha. This is between me and you and there's no need to cause a scene."

Tasha starts to push the stroller away and Michael reaches out for her. "Tasha, please wait I don't want our day to end like this."

Tasha touches Michael's face and says, "We had a fun time but you really need to handle your business with that thing. I'm too classy to fight and besides he ain't even worth it. Call me when you know what you wanna do."

Tasha pushes Mitchell away and glares at Jeffrey as she walks in front of him. Jeffrey starts to get louder and gets in Michael's face. His friends egg him on to fight.

Michael calmly says, "Jeff, you really don't wanna do this out here. Let's go home and talk about this."

Jeffrey pushes Michael. "Jeff, don't push me. I'm not playing with you." Jeffrey pushes Michael harder and he stumbles.

Michael shouts, "I don't wanna hurt you. Please don't push me again."

Jeffrey throws a punch instead of pushing Michael. Michael dodges the punch and throws one of his own. The two men begin to fight and a crowd rushes to see the commotion. As they fall to the dusty ground, security guards pull them apart and call the police to come and get them. Michael and Jeffrey are put in separate police

cars and are carted off to jail.
Michael is carried into the police
station and sits handcuffed to the
bench waiting to see the judge. All
he can think about is calling Tasha
to apologize for everything. A
police officer approaches Michael
and asks, "Is there anyone you can
call to post your bail and pick you
up?"

Michael says, "Yes, I need the
phone number out of my cell
phone." The officer breaks the rules
and allows Michael to use his cell
phone to call Tasha. Tasha arrived
home and placed the sleeping
Mitchell in his crib. Just as she
closes his door, her cell phone rings
and she runs to get it hoping it was
Michael. Seeing that it is her heart
leaps with excitement.

"Tasha, hey it's me. Can you do
me a favor please? I'm at the 25th
precinct downtown. Could you
come and post my bail please?"

Tasha is speechless and finally
gathers herself enough to say, "Yes,
I will come get you. Let me call
Paulie to watch Mitch, ok? I will be
there as soon as I can."

Tasha hangs up and calls Paulie.
"Girl, you will never guess what

happened at the carnival? Mike and I were having a ball and Jeffrey shows up with his queen friends and causes a scene. So, I left and apparently Jeffrey and Michael got in a fight. He's sitting in jail downtown. Could you get someone to cover for you really quick so I can get him please?"

Paulie says, "Yes and that's a hot mess. Two grown men acting like teenage boys fighting. You should let his butt stay in jail overnight. I'm on my way."

Paulie arrives to the house within fifteen minutes and Tasha dashes out the door. She pulls up to the police station and jumps out the car to run in after Michael. He sees her walking in looking frantic and he couldn't help to feel such a great peace with her there.

She comes up to him and gives him a hug. "Dang Mike, if you look like this I hate to see what Jeffrey looks like. He got you good."

Michael feels his lip and face knowing they are bruised. Tasha goes over to the counter to post the bail and they release Michael into her custody. Michael breathes a sigh of relief and says, "Thank you so much for coming to get me. I really hope this doesn't affect my career. This whole situation is a big mess. And, I can't go home tonight because I know he will be there. That will make me want to fight him again." He stops short and looks at the mother of his child. The love he feels for her overwhelms him and he wonders for the thousandth time how he could have hurt her.

"Uh, Tasha, could I please stay with you? I'm not trying to push up on you but I need to get some space and figure what I'm going to do next. Please. I have nowhere else to go."

Tasha sighs and says, "I really don't want to considering you did me wrong but I guess I will be nice today. You can sleep on the couch. But I need you gone in the morning."

Michael agrees and jumps in her car. Tasha pulls up in front of her house and Michael stands outside looking and thinking this should be the home he bought for her. She opens the door and he follows her in and takes his shoes off at her front door.

"Michael, do you want to take a shower? Cause you can't lay on my couch looking like that." They both laugh and Paulie comes out the room because she hears voices other than Tasha.

She sees Michael standing there bloody and bruised. Paulie lets out a big laugh and says, "Wow Mike, that dude whipped your ass!" Michael doesn't think Paulie's comments and laughter are very funny.

Michael says as he holds his face, "I guess I did have that coming to me huh?"

Tasha says, "You sure did. Now here's a towel and sheets for the couch. I will wake you up in the morning before I go to church so you can leave."

Paulie pointed to her eyes and says, "Don't be slick because I'm watching you. Goodnight."

Michael uses the guest bathroom to get cleaned up and comes out with only his boxers on after his shower. He sits on the couch and stares off into space. Tasha comes out when she hears the water stop running and brings some bandages and alcohol to clean his cuts. She also has an old pair of basketball shorts that she took from Michael.

"Here you go. These are your shorts that you gave me when we were in college. Let me clean your face up." As she rubbed the alcohol on his bruised face and hands, Michael closed his eyes and relaxed. She gently touches him and he laid his head back and falls asleep. She takes the blanket and covers him with it. Tasha gets up from the couch and stands over him. She finally allows herself to feel that love that she has in her heart. Before going into her room she whispers, "Goodnight, My Love."

Hearing the bedroom door close, Michael opens his eyes and says, "Goodnight, My Love." He smiles before drifting off to sleep for real this time.

STAY TUNED!

**Find out what happens to Michael
and Tasha in Surrendering to Love.
Summer 2013!**

Book T.T. Harris for your next event
by contacting:

thekeysproductions@gmail.com

www.thekeysproductions.com